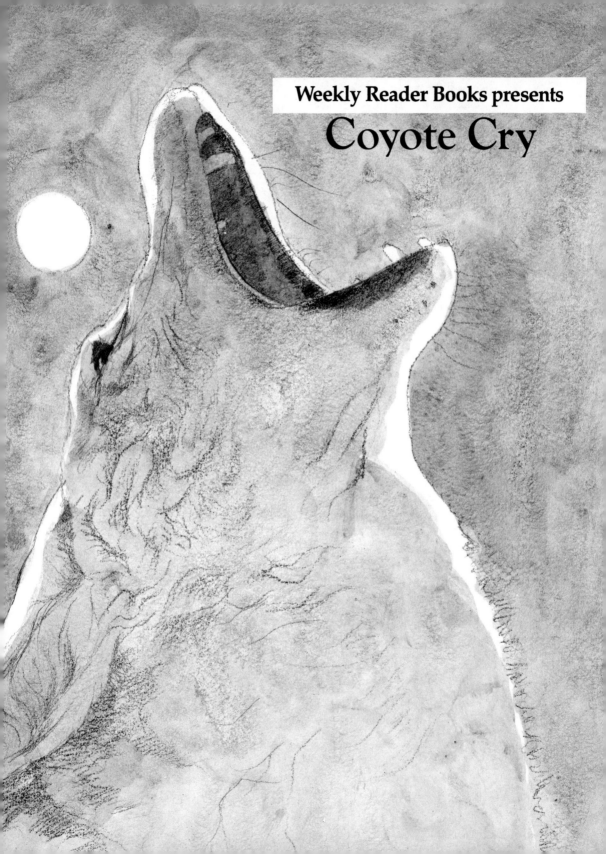

Weekly Reader Books presents

Coyote Cry

BYRD BAYLOR

COYOTE CRY

drawings by

SYMEON SHIMIN

Lothrop, Lee & Shepard Co. | New York

This book is a presentation of
Weekly Reader Books

Weekly Reader Books offers
book clubs for children from
preschool through junior high school.
All quality hardcover books are selected by
a distinguished Weekly Reader Selection Board.

For further information write to:
Weekly Reader Books
1250 Fairwood Ave.
Columbus, Ohio 43216

It is night.

A boy and an old man sit beside their campfire, listening, listening . . . waiting.

Finally, from somewhere across the hills, from some rocky ledge, from some steep ravine comes the high windy cry of a coyote.

At first they hear only one. But from other hills and other ledges and other ravines coyotes answer. Ay-eee. Ay-eee.

In the darkness, far back from the small, flickering campfire, coyotes sing and yip and howl and whine.

The boy, Antonio, stiffens.

He does not like that sound, that wailing, that yapping. And anyway, Coyote is his enemy. Antonio never forgets that, even at the end of a day, when he is almost ready for sleep.

"Coyote is my enemy," he says. "And I am his."

But the old man, the grandfather, has no enemies. Sometimes he even makes excuses for Coyote.

He says, "It is hard to enjoy a supper of rocks and sand, and so Coyote does what he must to stay alive."

"Even so, he is my enemy."

"He is our neighbor, our *compañero*," the grandfather says. "We share the same rocky land."

"Even so, he is my enemy."

The grandfather and the boy have nothing else to do now that the sheep are quiet in their night pen, now that the beans and green chiles and tortillas and wild honey have been eaten, now that the stars are out.

So they listen to coyotes.

"They have a different song tonight," the grandfather says after awhile. "It tells you there will be rain. Not tonight. Maybe not tomorrow either. But soon. Coyote feels a change in the air."

Antonio listens. He feels only the still dry summer night, yet he knows that his grandfather hears many things in the coyote's voice that he himself has not yet learned to hear.

The old man tries to teach the boy these things.

"Sometimes," he says, "Coyote sings for the coming of winter. Sometimes he sings for hunger or for thirst. Sometimes for his mate. Some people even say they know by his song whether he runs free in the hills or whether he fears traps and hunters."

"Let him fear *me*," Antonio says.

Sometimes Coyote seems to be laughing, not afraid of anything at all.

The old man has seen coyotes gathered together for company. He is sure of that.

"And they play games—those coyotes—chasing each other until they have to lie down, panting. I have looked at tracks that ran around and around. I almost think that on those nights Coyote dances."

But Antonio does not wish to think of Coyote dancing on some sandy ledge. Coyote is his enemy. He only thinks of him *that* way.

"He won't be dancing after he meets me. Then he'll be running. *Cuidado*, Coyote. *Cuidado*. Watch out for me."

It is like this every night.

The old man and the boy lie there on the ground, each with his blanket wrapped around him. They lie pressed as close to the earth as any of the wild creatures up in the hills. And when they sleep, they close their eyes, still listening to the coyotes, who have been hidden all day and now will walk their trails by moonlight.

Antonio and his grandfather cannot let themselves sleep soundly.

They sleep—they even dream—still half listening for the sheep they must take care of day and night.

Now, of course, the sheep are quiet. But their pen is no more than a wide circle of branches that Antonio and his grandfather cut from scrub oak and manzanita and sycamore trees. It is not high enough or strong enough to keep all other animals out.

If a wildcat prowls, if a night bird screeches, if a coyote comes close, the sheep will run in fear. If the sheep move,

the old man always wakes first, faster than Antonio, and he runs to the pen. He runs, calling out to calm his sheep. And his eyes peer into the shadows to find what it is they fear.

Too often it is Coyote he finds there. And Coyote must be kept away from the summer lambs, which still run, playing and jumping in the pen long after their mothers are quiet.

Usually, the long-haired yellow collie Blanca sleeps where she too can guard the sheep.

Like the old man, this dog's whole life, as far back as Antonio can remember, has been caring for that flock of sheep . . . herding them across the valley to graze, bringing them back in the evening, keeping them safe all through the night.

But now Blanca does not run beside the old man when they go down the trail in the morning. Neither does she stay beside the sheep at night, because she has four new pups hidden under a manzanita bush not far from the glow of the campfire. There, the small branches twist down and touch the earth and the pups lie curled together among the shadows, pale and soft.

They are still too young to open their eyes. They don't even have names yet . . . and they have no need of names. They have never left the manzanita branches that keep them hidden from the rest of the world. They have never been far from their mother's warm fur.

But now in the first gray half-light of dawn, the pups stir. One of them stretches and yawns and rolls away from the others until he lies beyond the shelter of the manzanita branches.

The old man, too, moves restlessly in his sleep. Even in sleep, he seems to know that something is not as it should be. Without opening his eyes, he lifts his head to listen.

There is nothing but silence—silence and crickets. He drifts back into sleep. . . .

It is the wild barking of the dog Blanca that rouses Antonio and the grandfather at sunrise. They leave their blankets and go running toward the manzanita, where Blanca is sniffing the ground, circling back and forth, growling.

Antonio kneels beside the pups, stroking them, whispering to them. "But you are all right. Nothing is wrong here. . . ."

And then he sees that one of the pups is gone.

"Coyote!" he screams out. "Coyote was here."

And he is right. Already the grandfather is bending over coyote tracks in the sand.

The tracks circle the manzanita bush. They tell of one coyote, alone, quiet as a shadow.

Antonio is angry, and his anger is loud. He fills the dawn with his shouts, with his threats. He wants every coyote in the hills to hear him.

"I'll get you, Coyote. *Cuidado,* Coyote. Watch out, Thief."

Even though it is still too dark to see far beyond the light of their lantern, they both search for the pup. Perhaps, after all, he has just crawled away. Perhaps the coyote tracks mean nothing.

But the grandfather says, "The pup made no tracks. No tracks at all."

He looks off toward the hills, shaking his head, wondering. . . .

There is only one hope—to find where these coyote tracks lead. This will be Antonio's job.

While the old man takes the sheep to pasture, the boy follows the tracks from the small twisting tree, past the sheep pen, along the damp sandy creek and up toward the first hills. But now the earth becomes rocky. Time after time, Antonio sits down on the ground and studies the faint footprints, trying to decide which way to turn.

Often the ground is too hard to hold a footprint. Or grass may hide it. Or there may be only rocks.

Antonio stops to listen. Even the slightest voice could tell him something. But the wind carries no coyote sounds today, no pup sounds. Only quail flutter from the tall shadowy grass as he walks by. Only jack rabbits watch him from the far hills.

And when he calls out "I'll get you, Coyote!" there is only an echo of his own small voice in the ravine: "I'll get you, Coyote."

But he does not get Coyote. All that afternoon, he does not even see Coyote.

Instead, he walks slowly back to meet the grandfather as he brings the sheep to their evening watering place in the shallow creek. The old man doesn't have to ask. He sees Antonio's face and he knows.

For a long time, they don't talk about it at all. They simply go about the business of caring for the sheep. And then Antonio chops wood while the grandfather cooks beans on the open fire.

It is not until night, when once more they lie on the ground, wrapped in their blankets, that Antonio can talk about it.

And then the grandfather says, "Of course, it is possible that the little one was not harmed."

But Antonio will not be comforted. "Coyote is mean," he says. "He is my enemy and I am his."

"Remember," the grandfather reminds him, "we saw no sign that Coyote killed the pup."

Antonio shakes his head in the darkness. "I saw enough. I know."

It is always this way at night now. When the coyotes wail softly in the far hills, the old man and the boy lie beside the last glow of their campfire and talk about how different it would have been if only one of them had been awake when Coyote came creeping into their camp . . . or they talk about what the tracks looked like that morning, circling the manzanita's lowest branches.

"By studying those tracks," the old man says, "I know that Coyote was a female, small and light herself."

They think this over.

"Then why didn't she have pups of her own? Why wasn't she taking care of them instead of stealing another one? Why did she leave her den?"

They can only wonder about these things. Night under the summer stars is a time for wondering.

During the days, when they are out with the sheep they do not speak of it, but each one knows that they both half believe they will find the answer somewhere in one of those dry ravines, or in some grassy flat, or along some quiet trail.

Every day Antonio thinks, we could find that answer any day, this day, tomorrow. When?

Now it is morning—another morning.

Antonio and his grandfather have taken the sheep a different way this time, along the other side of the creek. They have just walked across a little hill and they stop to rest near the bottom of the slope.

There has been rain and the air is cool and the far blue mountains seem closer. The grandfather bends down to look at a cactus flower blossoming pink and white from a crack in a rock.

Just below them at the foot of the hill, the rock juts out and forms a shelter, a small overhang not large enough to call a cave. The boy and the old man stand for a minute here on the slope of the hill, looking down. They are not in a hurry.

Something moves. They see a flash of yellow fur among the tall weeds. Antonio hardly breathes. The grandfather is as still as a rock or a tree. They wait.

Below them the small furry thing moves back into the rock shelter and then again comes bounding into the sunlight.

Now they are sure. It is the pup . . . Blanca's pup.

Antonio wants to run to it at once. But the old man puts out his hand to stop him. They stay there, watching.

Now something else comes into sight. A coyote—a mother coyote—puts her forepaw against the pup and plays with him the way any mother dog plays with her own babies. The pup rolls and nips and jumps. The coyote watches him. She turns her head from side to side whenever the pup moves.

When the pup is tired and flops down in the sand to rest, she licks its fur and nuzzles it. The pup makes its small contented sounds.

But Antonio's hands are tight. His eyes blink. He cannot believe what he is seeing. It is as if the hills he has walked all his life had turned suddenly into a strange and unknown land.

"Coyote," Antonio whispers. "Coyote. . . ."

Antonio does not wait to see what the grandfather wants to do. He goes leaping across the rocks to the bottom of the hill.

At the first sound, the coyote and the collie pup both run toward the rock shelter. There, the pup has been carefully taught, is safety. But Antonio is beside him in an instant. He grabs the pup up into his arms.

The coyote looks at the pup but there is nothing she can do to hide him now. She turns and runs, and Antonio, holding the pup tightly against him, sees the coyote look back before she disappears in the low brush. The pup whines and tries to twist loose, but Antonio says, "No, stay with us. You're no coyote."

The old man is there now. Together they look at the coyote's den, the damp earth, the grass bent to fit the creatures that lay there, the rocks that almost hid them from sight.

From far away there comes a coyote's cry. The pup turns its head and yelps.

The coyote sound comes once more, farther away, as lonely as any sound you ever heard. Antonio keeps it in his mind even after it has stopped.

They take the pup and turn back to the sheep, and all that day Antonio keeps the pup with him. His mind whirls with his own thoughts, with the sharp puppy barks beside him, with the memory of that voice.

"Why?" he keeps asking the grandfather as they walk beside the sheep. "Why did that coyote take Blanca's pup if not to kill him?"

The old man, of course, can only guess. "Maybe something happened to her own pups. Maybe she kept looking for them. Maybe she kept wishing for another one."

"She must have been afraid when she came to our camp."

The old man nods. "But Coyote does what it must. It does what its bones say to do."

Late in the afternoon, they bring the sheep back to the creek for water and then up the bank to their pen.

Antonio runs ahead and takes the pup to Blanca. Blanca sniffs the pup and bristles and walks around him, looking at him carefully. She smells the touch of coyote on her pup and it puzzles her. Like Antonio, Blanca has been at war with coyotes for a long time. Yet, finally, she decides to take the pup back and she pushes him toward his brothers.

The pups no longer stay under the manzanita branches. Now they are old enough, strong enough, to come out into the world, to explore, to taste, to blink in the sunlight, to jump at Antonio.

Antonio watches the pup he has just carried home from the coyote's den. It is a dog again, not a coyote. Yet he

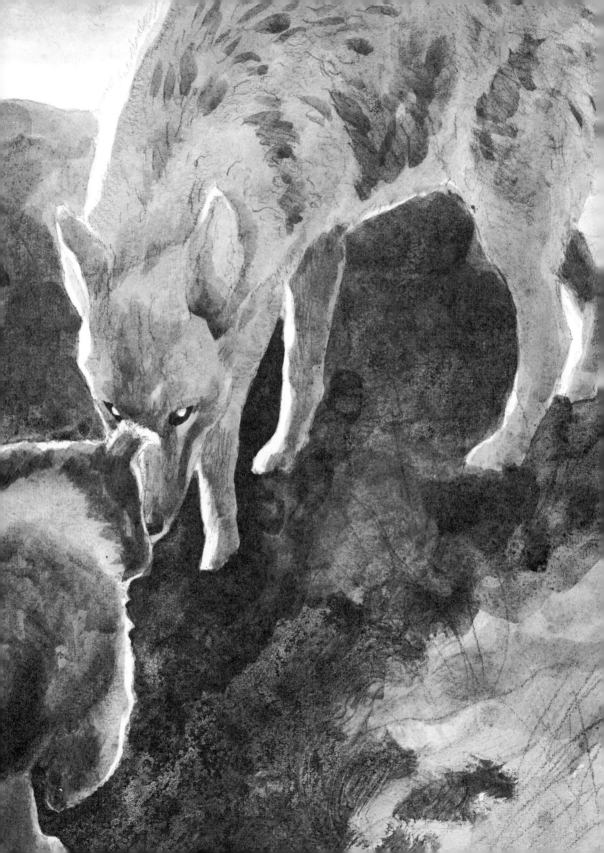

wonders. . . . When it grows up will it remember anything of those days? Will the sound of a coyote cry mean
anything to him? Will he remember a den hidden among
the rocks?

The old man and the boy listen carefully at night. Who
knows whether the coyote will come back? Perhaps she is
waiting in the shadows. Perhaps she will try to take the
pup again. . . .

But that night passes. And another. And another.

And they put it out of their minds.

Then one cool dawn—still dark but with the first
streaks of orange in the night sky—the old man lifts his
head from his blanket. He sees two eyes shining. It is
Coyote. He reaches over and touches Antonio, and puts his
finger to his lips. "Shhh."

They make no sound.

Now they see the pup moving toward the spot where
Coyote stands. Coyote comes no closer. She waits. The
pup peers into the darkness to make sure. Then he goes to
the coyote and they touch noses. That is all. Just that. The
pup goes back to his sleeping brothers.

When they look again, Coyote is gone.

She does not come back.

They know her tracks now, and every day they search for them around the camp. But she does not come back.

Yet even now that summer is past, the old man and the boy remember her.

They still lie under the stars, listening, listening as they always have for the night's first faraway coyote song.

Ay-eee.

And then they wait for other voices to come from the moonlit hills, from the deep canyons.

Ay-eee. Ay-eee.

Could one of the voices be *that* one?

"When she comes back again, that coyote . . . I'll give her something for supper. A melon, if we have it." Antonio says. "You saw how skinny she was."

"A melon for your enemy?" the grandfather asks, surprised.

"Maybe Coyote is not my enemy now," Antonio says very softly.

And then after awhile, it seems to him that the coyote voices have changed. He hears in them now a sound he must never have noticed before.

It is a song that coyotes sing only to the moon. You hear it only when the moon is yellow and low.

The boy knows suddenly what that song is about. He *knows.*

It is about being alive. It is about this rocky land, these windy hills where Coyote runs.

So Antonio says, "Someday I will be one of those people who can tell you what things Coyote is saying."

And the coyote song rises to the moon.

Ay-eee. Ay-eee.